WHOO

Meg was meeting
Bess, Jess, Tess and Cress

374328

MOG'S MISSING

by

and J

ski

PUFFIN BOOKS

He wanted to go hunting

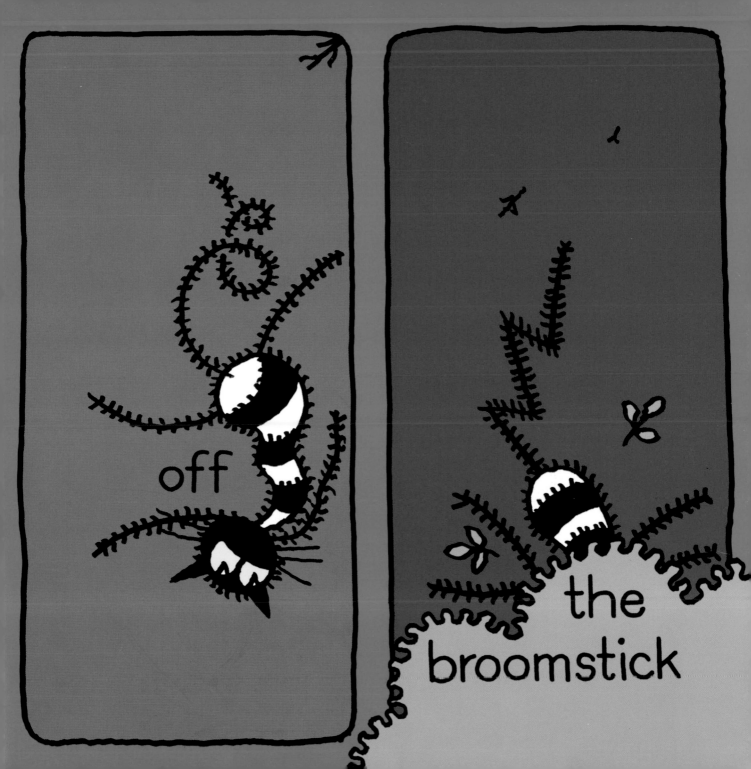

They met

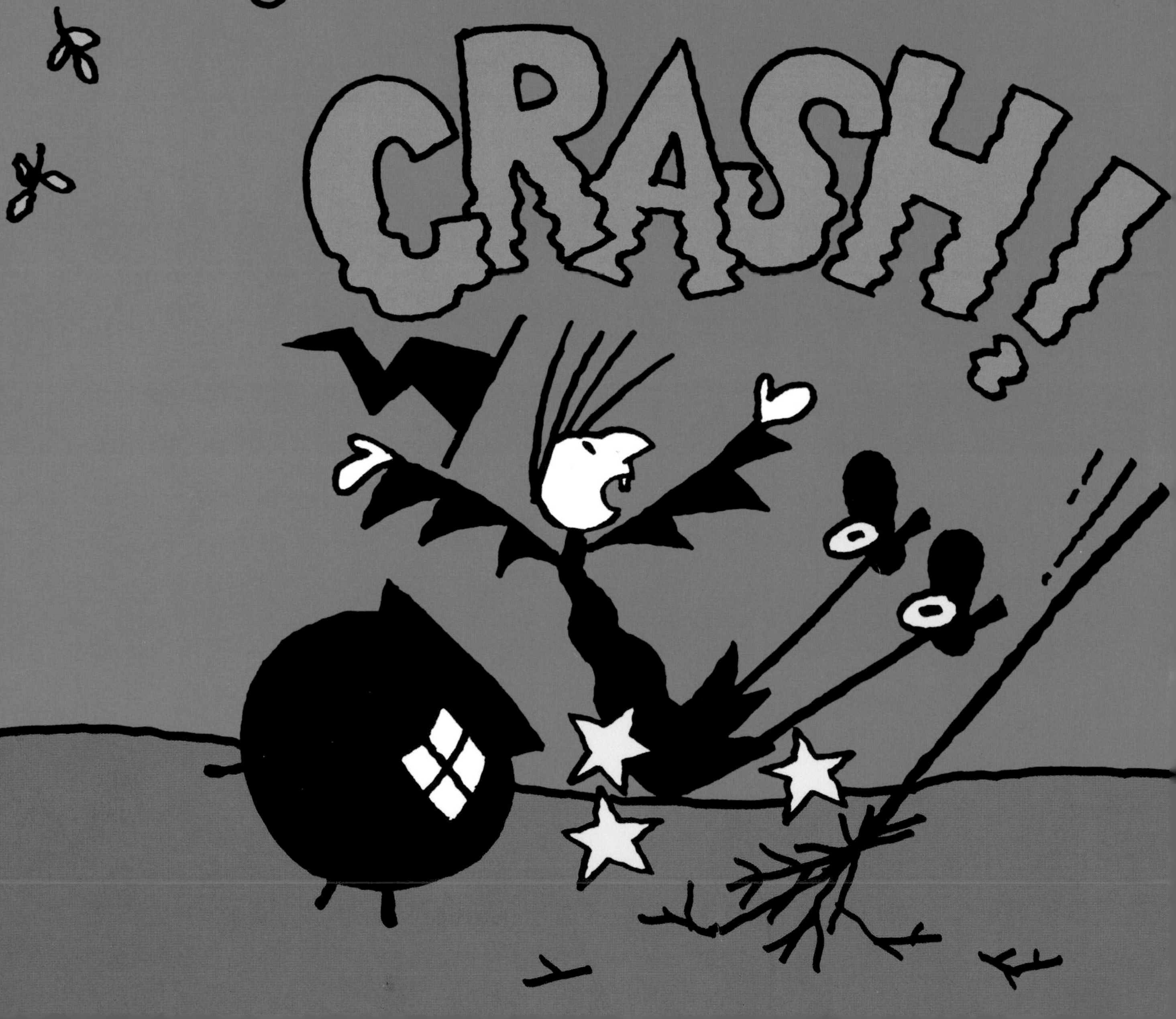

They made up a search party

Mog was not up the ash tree

He was not in the hollow oak

He was not down a rabbit hole

They couldn't find him anywhere

BANG
CLANG

MIAOW!

They were all in the cauldron

with Mog

Meg and Mog flew home

and had breakfast

Goodbye!

for Yacine, Hédi and Sherif

PUFFIN BOOKS

Published by the Penguin Group: London, New York, Australia, Canada, India, Ireland, New Zealand and South Africa

Penguin Books Ltd, Registered Offices: 80 Strand, London WC2R 0RL, England

puffinbooks.com

First published 2005

Published in this edition 2007

10 9 8 7 6 5 4

Text copyright © Helen Nicoll, 2005

Illustrations copyright © Jan Pieńkowski, 2005

Story and characters copyright © Helen Nicoll and Jan Pieńkowski, 2005

All rights reserved

The moral right of the author and illustrator has been asserted

Lettering by Caroline Austin

Made and printed in China by Leo Paper Group

British Library Cataloguing in Publication Data

A CIP catalogue record for this book is available from the British Library

ISBN: 978-0-141-50024-9